S0-CYF-357

This book belongs to

....

Quarto is the authority on a wide range of topics.

Quarto educates, entertains and enriches the lives of our readers—enthusiasts and lovers of hands-on living.

www.quartoknows.com

© 2019 Quarto Publishing plc

First published in 2019 by QEB Publishing, an imprint of The Quarto Group.
6 Orchard Road, Suite 100
Lake Forest, CA 92630
T: +1 949 380 7510
F: +1 949 380 7575
www.QuartoKnows.com

All rights reserved. No part of this publication may be reproduced, stored in a retrieval system, or transmitted in any form or by any means, electronic, mechanical, photocopying, recording, or otherwise, without the prior permission of the publisher, nor be otherwise circulated in any form of binding or cover other than that in which it is published and without a similar condition being imposed on the subsequent purchaser.

A CIP record for this book is available from the Library of Congress.

ISBN 978-0-7112-4939-4

Based on the original story by Jessica Barrah and Chris Saunders
Author of adapted text: Katie Woolley
Series Editor: Joyce Bentley
Series Designer: Sarah Peden

Manufactured in Guangdong, China TT012020
9 8 7 6 5 4 3 2 1

MIX
Paper from responsible sources
FSC® C016973

**Reading
Gems**

The Helpful
DRAGON

The people of Puddle Town had a problem.
It was a large, red, fiery problem.

"There's a dragon on the tracks," shouted
the stationmaster.

All the people tried to wake it up,
but nothing they did worked.

The dragon just snored and snored.

The people gathered in the town square for a meeting.

"There will be a reward for anyone who can move that dragon," said the mayor.

One little girl knew just what to do.

Lucy rode to the train station as fast as she could.

"I want that reward, so that I can buy a new bike," she said. "I'll move the dragon."

The red, fiery dragon was very, very big! Lucy decided that it must be hungry.

"Would you like some food, Mr. Dragon?" she asked. Lucy rustled a little bag of potato chips.

Potato chips were the dragon's favorite snack. He opened one eye.

"Yes, please!" he said. "I am a little bit hungry."

The dragon ate all the chips in one big gulp! Snap! Snap! Snap!

The trouble was that he was a big dragon.

"I'm still hungry," he said. "Can I have some more food, please?"

"Follow me," said Lucy. "I'm sure we can find some more in the town."

The dragon got up off the tracks, and the pair went to look for food.

They went to the park. Some people were having a picnic. The grass was too wet, and the food was getting soggy. The people gave the dragon some cake.

Then, Lucy had an idea! She whispered in the dragon's ear.

The dragon quickly breathed hot air over the grass. It was soon dry.

He gobbled up some more food, but the dragon was still hungry.

Lucy and the dragon went to find more food. Nearby, a chef was cooking on a barbecue, but he didn't have any fire.

"I know what to do!" said Lucy. She whispered in the dragon's ear again.

Quick as a flash, the dragon breathed fire over the barbecue. It was soon sizzling!

Then, he ate a sausage or two! But the dragon was still hungry.

They kept going. Lucy and the dragon walked into a wedding party. There was lots of food to eat. The dragon licked his lips!

"Hello," said the bride. "I'll give you some food if you warm up my wedding tent."

"Of course!" said the dragon.

He breathed hot air into the tent until it was warm and cozy.

Then, he gobbled up all the cupcakes.

Back at the town square, it was time for the fair.

Lucy's mother had come to the fair to see where Lucy was.

"I'm here!" said Lucy. She and the dragon had come to join the fun at the fair. "The dragon is right here, too!"

"Gosh, what a big dragon!" said the mayor.

"Don't worry," said Lucy. "He's a helpful dragon!"

"What a helpful dragon!" said the mayor.
"Will you stay in Puddle Town?"

"Yes, please," said the dragon.
"I like it here."

The dragon had great fun at
the fair. He ate all the food.
He even ate Lucy's doughnut!

He lit the village fireworks.
Whiz! Pop! Bang!

"Hooray for the helpful
dragon!" cried the people.

Story Words

barbecue

bike

breathed

bride

chef

chips

dragon

fireworks

food

mayor

reward

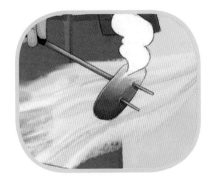

sausage

stationmaster

tracks

wedding

Let's Talk About
The Helpful Dragon

Look carefully at the book cover.

Who is in the picture?

What is the dragon doing?

Name some of the food that the dragon is eating.

The dragon is very hungry in the story. He likes to eat all kinds of food.

What food do you like to eat? What is your favorite meal? Is there anything you don't like?

The dragon turns out to be helpful.

Can you remember how he helps the people of Puddle Town?

Lucy decides to move the dragon away from the train tracks.

Why does she do this? Do you think she got her reward?

Did you like the ending of the story?

What do you think happened next?

Fun and Games

Look back through the story, and put these characters in the order they appear.

bride

dragon

Lucy

mayor

stationmaster

chef

Answers: 1—stationmaster; 2—dragon; 3—mayor; 4—Lucy; 5—chef; and 6—bride.

Say these words out loud. Does the letter pattern in bold of each pair sound the same or different?

a

dr**a**gon

st**a**tion

b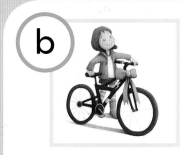

b**i**k**e**

br**i**d**e**

c

p**air**

f**air**

d

f**i**re

ch**i**ps

Answers: a–no; b–yes; c–yes; and d–no.

Your Turn

Now that you have read the story,
try telling it in your own words.
Use the pictures below to help you.

31

READING TOGETHER

- When reading this book together, suggest that your child looks at the pictures to help them make sense of any words they are unsure about, and ask them to point to any letters they recognize.

- Try asking questions such as, "Can you break the word into parts?" and "Are there clues in the picture that help you?"

- During the story, ask your child questions such as, "Can you remember what has happened so far?" and "What do you think will happen next?"

- Look at the story words on pages 24–25 together. Encourage your child to find the pictures and the words on the story pages, too.

- There are lots of activities you can play at home with your child to help them with their reading. Write the alphabet onto 26 cards, and hide them around the house. Encourage your child to shout out the letter name when they find a card!

- In the car, play "I Spy" to help your child learn to recognize the first sound in a word.

- Organize a family read-aloud session once a week! Each family member chooses something to read out loud. It could be their favorite book, a magazine, a menu, or the back of a food package.

- Give your child lots of praise, and take great delight when your child successfully sounds out a new word.

Level 4